Mary, Mary, quite contrary,
How does your garden grow?
With silver bells,
And cockleshells,
And pretty maids all in a row.

For Suzanne: every garden should have such a splendid bloom
—A.McQ.

To Ethan and Frankie with love
—R.B.

 Find the Lulu Loves Flowers cover colouring-in page and more
on our website. Scan the code to download or visit the activity page on
our website, www.alannamax.com

Published in the UK & Ireland by Alanna Max
38 Oakfield Road, London N4 4NL
Lulu Loves Flowers © 2021 Alanna Max
Text copyright © 2015 Anna McQuinn
Illustrations copyright © 2015 Rosalind Beardshaw
Lulu Loves Flowers is part of the Booky Girl Lulu series
developed by and published under licence from Anna McQuinn.
www.AnnaMcQuinn.com

All Rights Reserved.
www.AlannaMax.com

Printed in China
ISBN 978-1-907825-286 HB
ISBN 978-1-907825-293 PB

Lulu Loves Flowers

Anna McQuinn

Illustrated by Rosalind Beardshaw

Alanna Max

Lulu loves her book of garden poems.
Her favourite is the one about Mary Mary.

Lulu wants a flower garden too.
Mummy says there's space near
her vegetables.

Lulu gets books about gardens
from the library.

She chooses her favourite flowers
from the books.

Mummy writes them in a list.

They go to the garden centre
to buy seeds.

Lulu and Mummy plant the seeds.

The packets mark where each flower
is planted.

Lulu checks next day, but she can't see any flowers yet.

She will have to wait a long time for them to grow.

While she waits, Lulu makes her own flower book.

Mummy types the Mary Mary poem
and Lulu glues it in.

Lulu makes a string of bells.
She finds shells and some old beads.

She even makes
a little Mary Mary!

One day, Lulu sees tiny green shoots!

She pulls up weeds
so the shoots can grow.

As the weather gets warmer,
Lulu's flowers open up to the sun.

Daddy helps Lulu hang her shiny bells.

She puts her shells and beads in a row
and finds a special spot for Mary Mary.
It's just perfect!

Orla, Ben and Tayo are coming
to see Lulu's garden.
Lulu and Mummy make cupcakes.

Lulu puts on her favourite flower top
and Mummy helps do her hair.

Lulu's friends love everything about her garden.

They share the crunchy peas
and sweet strawberries
that Mummy grew.

Then Lulu decides to make up a new story about Mary Mary.

What will Lulu think of next!

Lulu, Lulu, extraordinary,
How does your garden grow?
With flower seeds,
And shells and beads,
And happy friends all in a row.